LITTLE BOY WITH A
BIG HORN

by Jack Bechdolt

pictures by Aurelius Battaglia

A Golden Book • New York
Golden Books Publishing Company, Inc.
New York, New York 10106

Ollie was learning to play the bass horn.
Ollie was a small boy. And the horn was a big horn.

He knew only one tune. It was called "Asleep in the Deep."
It told about a shipwreck and brave sailors.
Maybe you know that tune.
The music goes way down deep, like this:
"MANY
 BRAVE HEARTS
  ARE ASLEEP IN
   THE DEEP SO
    BEWARE
      BEEEEE
        E
         E
          E
           E
            E
             WARE!"

Ollie loved that song, but...
Ollie's mother said, "Please, NOT in the house, Ollie.
It's too LOUD!"

"Yes, Mother," said Ollie and took his horn
into the back yard.
    "*Beeeeee-ware . . . BEEEEWARE!*"
boomed the big horn.

"*Owrooool!*" howled all the town dogs.

"Oh bother!" said all the neighbors.

"MANY
     BRAVE HEARTS
          ARE ASLEEP IN
               THE DEEP SO BEWARE
                    BEEEEE
                         E
                          E
                           E
                            E
                             E
                              WARE!"

The Grocer dropped a crate of eggs.

The Preacher couldn't write his sermon.

The Farmer's horses ran away.

Everybody agreed that the town must do something to
stop Ollie from playing that horn.

All together they called on Ollie's mother.

"We love music," they said, "but too much is TOO
MUCH!"

"But the boy must practice," said Ollie's mother.

"Perhaps, but not here," said the neighbors.

"We must think of a better place," said Ollie's mother.

"Yes, yes, a better place," they all agreed. "But where?"

Everyone thought hard.

"I have it," Ollie cried.

Everybody stopped thinking and looked at him.

"I'll go way off in the fields. Nobody can hear me there."

"Splendid!" said everybody.

"Wonderful idea!" they agreed.

"Ollie is a good boy," said his proud mother.

Ollie set out for the distant pastures.
The sun was hot.
He grew tired. But he kept on.

Far from home, he stopped at last.
He spread out his music and took up his horn.
First he played, "Unk. . . unk. . . UNK."

Then he played "Asleep in the Deep."
Surely nobody would mind now, for there was
nobody to mind!
But somebody did mind!
Over the hill the Farmer's cows were grazing.

"Beeeee-WARE!" boomed the big horn.

The cattle raised their heads.

They had never heard the likes of it. They began to gather from near and far. They began to move toward the strange noise.

"**Mooo!**" said one.

"**Arooo!**" bawled another.

The busy Farmer heard them.

"Drat," he said. "The old muley has fallen into the ditch again."

Pitchfork in hand, he came running to rescue his cows.

When he saw Ollie, the Farmer was angry.

"You can't play that horn here," he said. "It's enough to sour their milk."

"Oh, dear," sighed Ollie.

He picked up his horn and turned homeward.
The sun shone hot on his back.
He was thirsty. And tired.
"Seems as if there is no place in the world where
I can learn to play my horn," he sighed.

And then he had another bright idea.
Far off he saw the ocean.
"I'll go down to the ocean," said Ollie. "There's nobody
there but fish and seagulls, and they won't mind my music."

So he went and got his rowboat and began to row far out from the shore.

Some dangerous rocks marked the entrance to the harbor.

The rocks were guarded by a bell buoy that tolled a warning to incoming vessels.

But when Ollie reached the rocks, the bell buoy
was not there. It had drifted away.
There was nothing to warn the vessels.

And now a thick fog was spreading over the ocean.
It shut out sight of everything, even the rocks near by.
Every day at this time a steamship brought passengers and
freight to the town where Ollie lived.

The ship must be somewhere near even now,
lost in the fog.

There was no warning bell to tell its captain
when he was near the rocks.

The ship might strike on the reef.
"I'll stay here and play on my horn," Ollie decided.
"That will be a warning."

So Ollie stayed. And he played.

He played "Asleep in the Deep," because that was the only tune he knew.

A big gray gull circled over his head. Then another.
And another.

"**Awk-awk-awk-awk**," they shouted angrily.

Some seals that lived on the rocks began to bark a protest,
"Owk—owk—owk!"

"I am very sorry if you don't like my music," said Ollie politely, "but I'm NOT going away."

He kept right on playing to warn the lost ship of her danger.

The ship was drawing closer.
The captain peered through the fog.

He and his crew could see nothing.

They listened for the bell buoy's warning. They could hear nothing but the sea.

But what was that noise?

"Bee-WARE!" boomed Ollie's big horn.

The men on the ship were amazed.

"Stop the ship," cried the Captain. "Lower a boat and find out what's making music out here on the ocean."

And that was how they found Ollie and escaped being wrecked upon the rocks.

"We owe our lives to this brave boy," said the steamship Captain.
All the passengers cheered.

When the ship reached her dock, all the town heard
of Ollie's brave deed.

"He must be rewarded," they said.

And a big public meeting was held at the Town Hall.

The Mayor gave Ollie a handsome medal marked
"FOR BRAVERY"
—and said the town would send Ollie to music school.

Ollie thanked the Mayor.
"I will be able to play my horn as much as I like," he said.
"And the school is so far from our town that nobody will be
disturbed any more."

And they weren't!